GREEN TIGER'S ILLUSTRATED

Stories from Shakespeare

MIDSUMMER NIGHTS DREAM
THE TEMPEST • AS YOU LIKE IT • TWELFTH NIGHT
MUCH ADO ABOUT NOTHING
TWO GENTLEMAN OF VERONA
ALL WELLS THAT ENDS WELL
THE COMEDY OF ERRORS • TAMING OF THE SHREW

As told by E. Nesbit

Compiled by Benjamin Darling

GREEN TIGER PRESS • MMXI

COVER • ARTHUR RACKHAM, 1908.

HALF TITLE • UNKNOWN. POSTCARD, C. 1900.

FRONTISPIECE • MAX BIHN, 1907.

ENDPAPERS • A.E. JACKSON, C. 1930

GREEN TIGER PRESS

A DIVISION OF LAUGHING ELEPHANT

www.LAUGHINGELEPHANT.com

Preface

WHY SHAKESPEARE? Why indeed? Why literature whose authorship is dubious, written 400 years ago in dense and difficult language? Why should we share him with our children? Is he not inappropriate, archaic, and irrelevant? In short, why should we care? "Because I said said so" is the answer your parents might have given you. Your teachers will have added some words of wisdom about cultural literacy and "the classics" - and as we know from Mark Twain "the classics" are "Something that everybody wants to have read and nobody wants to read."

"BY ANY OTHER NAME WOULD SMELL AS SWEET" Regarding the importance of Shakespeare, C.A. Gaskell in the introduction to the Art Edition of the Most Popular Dramas From Shakespeare tells us in no uncertain terms that 'Next to the Bible and Pilgrim's Progress, no Classic of English Literature is more reverently esteemed by English speaking people than the works of William Shakespeare, So extensively have the characters of Shakespeare been drawn upon by artists, poets and writers of fiction—so interwoven are these characters in the great body of English literature, that to be ignorant of the plot of these dramas is often a cause for embarrassment and regret' The words of the unheralded C.A. Gaskell are no less true today, than when he (or she) wrote them in 1890. One need only consider Romeo and Juliet to prove this point. Nearly everyone knows that Romeo and Juliet are "star crossed lovers" who suffer and die for their love . So ingrained is this in our culture that other works as diverse as West Side Story, High School Musical and a number of Looney Tunes cartoons refer to it with the confidence that we all know what they are referring to, without need of elaboration. This and many other scenes, characters, phrases and words from the works of Shakespeare have become cultural shorthand that can, by briefly alluding to them, in an instant convey a whole range of meanings. "The Simpsons" have done not one but two Shakespeare themed episodes, and Hollywood has recently adapted Othello and The Taming of the Shrew into films aimed at teenagers. Shakespeare is vital still, and to be ignorant of his work is, as C.A. Gaskell points out, "cause for regret and embarrassment," or at the very least confusion as to why Foghorn Leghorn is standing on a balcony wearing a wig.

"TO THINE OWN SELF BE TRUE" In her introduction to the excellent Beautiful Stories From Shakespeare (from whence we have adapted our the text for this book) the renowned English children's author, E. Nesbit, tells her readers that "His plays alone (leaving mere science out of the question), contain more actual wisdom than the whole body of English learning. He is the teacher of all good—pity, generosity, true courage, love." Some might suggest that there is a bit of hyperbole in this statement but, laying "mere science" to one side as Nesbit recommends, it is not hard to see that the whole range of human emotions are contained in Shakespeare's plays if one takes the time to study them and to untangle some of the more arcane language. Even more amazing than their scope, however, is the humanity of Shakespeare's work. Every character is sympathetic, or at the very least empathetic; we can see why they feel the way they do and thus gain great insight into ourselves and perhaps more importantly, into others, even others we do not understand or even like.   A short list of quotes from the Bard on the human condition is enough to prove this point, and to emphasize again how deeply ingrained Shakespeare is in our lexicon:

ON LOVE: *"Parting is such sweet sorrow."* Romeo and Juliet
"But love is blind..." The Merchant of Venice

ON JEALOUSY: *"O, beware, my lord, of jealousy; It is the green-eyed monster..."* Othello
"How many fond fools serve mad jealousy!" The Comedy of Errors

ON KINDNESS: *"The quality of mercy is not strained."* The Merchant of Venice
"Yet do I fear thy nature; It is too full o' the milk of human kindness." Macbeth

ON ADVERSITY: *"Thus conscience does make cowards of us all."* Hamlet
"Misery acquaints a man with strange bedfellows." The Tempest
"The better part of valor is, discretion." Henry IV, Part I
"Neither a borrower nor a lender be." Hamlet

We could go on until we had exhausted the entire Shakespearean oeuvre and the whole range of human experience, but "brevity is the soul of wit" and more importantly of book introductions. Read! See! Enjoy!

"AS MERRY AS THE DAY IS LONG" One final answer to the question "why Shakespeare?" (there are many more answers to this excellent question than we can possibly answer here) is one that is barely hinted at in our opening paragraph—that Shakespeare is enjoyable! More than just enjoyable he is funny, fall down on the ground, clutch your sides, and try to catch your breath funny. When Malvolio in Twelfth Night, comes prancing out dressed in his yellow garters, there needs to be a pause in the play whilst the audience howls with laughter so loud one could not hear the actors speak. What we have said, and the examples we have given, could be repeated for every subject in Shakespeare's oeuvre, from comedy to history to tragedy. From low humor to high thought, from tears to laughter it is all there. That this abundant talent comes to us, as it does in Shakespeare's case, from a 400 year old text and that it is still so widely appealing is a cause for celebration.

"A POOR THING BUT MINE OWN" The language of Shakespeare can be a little hard to understand at first (though one does adapt very quickly) therefore a plot outline can be a helpful tool for children in attending plays. A simple grasp of the plot and main characters in the drama gives the first time viewer a bit of a head start and allows them to focus on the words and meaning of the play itself. That is in short the purpose of this book. In making it we have used E. Nesbit's excellent text, with very slight modifications for the modern reader, and illustrated it richly for aid and entertainment.   Nesbit said of her work that it was her goal "To reproduce the entertaining stories contained in the plays of Shakespeare, in a form so simple that children can understand and enjoy them." We humbly concur, and hope children and parents will find this book useful in beginning or enriching an appreciation of Shakespeare.

—Benjamin Darling

TABLE OF CONTENTS

As You Like It

Illustrations by Hugh Thomson, c. 1910

There was once a wicked Duke named Frederick, who took the dukedom that should have belonged to his brother, sending him into exile. His brother went into the Forest of Arden, where he lived the life of a bold forester, as Robin Hood did in Sherwood Forest in merry England.

The banished Duke's daughter, Rosalind, remained with Celia, Frederick's daughter, and the two loved each other more than most sisters. One day there was a wrestling match at Court, and Rosalind and Celia went to see it. Charles, a celebrated wrestler, was there, who had killed many men in contests of this kind. Orlando, the young man he was to wrestle with, was so slender and youthful, that Rosalind and Celia thought he would surely be killed, as others had been; so they spoke to him, and asked him not to attempt so dangerous an adventure; but the only effect of their words was to make him wish more to come off well in the encounter, so as to win praise from such sweet ladies.

Orlando, like Rosalind's father, was being kept out of his inheritance by his brother, and was so sad at his brother's unkindness that, until he saw Rosalind, he did not care much whether he lived or died. But now the sight of the fair Rosalind gave him strength and courage, so that he did marvelously, and at last, threw Charles to such a tune, that the wrestler had to be carried off the ground. Duke Frederick was pleased with his courage, and asked his name.

"My name is Orlando, and I am the youngest son of Sir Rowland de Boys," said the young man.

Now Sir Rowland de Boys, when he was alive, had been a good friend to the banished Duke, so that Frederick heard with regret whose son Orlando was, and would not befriend him. But Rosalind was delighted to hear that this handsome young stranger was the son of her father's old friend, and as they were going away, she turned back more than once to say another kind word to the brave young man.

"Gentleman," she said, giving him a chain from her neck, "wear this for me. I could give more, but that my hand lacks means."

Rosalind and Celia, when they were alone, began to talk about the handsome wrestler, and Rosalind confessed that she loved him at first sight.

"Come, come," said Celia, "wrestle with thy affections."

"Oh," answered Rosalind, "they take the part of a better wrestler than myself. Look, here comes the Duke."

"With his eyes full of anger," said Celia.

"You must leave the Court at once," he said to Rosalind. "Why?" she asked.

"Never mind why," answered the Duke, "you are banished. If within ten days you are found within twenty miles of my Court, you die."

So Rosalind set out to seek her father, the banished Duke, in the Forest of Arden. Celia loved her too much to let her go alone, and as it was rather a dangerous journey, Rosalind, being the taller, dressed up as a young countryman, and her cousin as a country girl, and Rosalind said that she would be called Ganymede, and Celia, Aliena. They were very tired when at last they came to the Forest of Arden, and as they were sitting on the grass a countryman passed that way, and Ganymede asked him if he could get them food. He did so, and told them that a shepherd's flocks and house were to be sold. They bought these and settled down as shepherd and shepherdess in the forest.

In the meantime, Oliver having sought to take his brother Orlando's life, Orlando also wandered into the forest, and there met with the rightful Duke, and being kindly received, stayed with him. Now, Orlando could think of nothing but Rosalind, and he went about the forest carving her name on trees, and writing love sonnets and hanging them on the bushes, and there Rosalind and Celia found them. One day Orlando met them, but he did not know Rosalind in her boy's clothes, though he liked the pretty shepherd youth, because he fancied a likeness in him to her he loved.

"There is a foolish lover," said Rosalind, "who haunts these woods and hangs sonnets on the trees. If I could find him, I would soon cure him of his folly."

Orlando confessed that he was the foolish lover, and Rosalind said—"If you will come and see me every day, I will pretend to be Rosalind, and I will take her part, and be wayward

and contrary, as is the way of women, till I make you ashamed of your folly in loving her."

And so every day he went to her house, and took a pleasure in saying to her all the pretty things he would have said to Rosalind; and she had the fine and secret joy of knowing that all his love-words came to the right ears. Thus many days passed pleasantly away.

One morning, as Orlando was going to visit Ganymede, he saw a man asleep on the ground, and that there was a lioness crouching near, waiting for the man who was asleep to wake: for they say that lions will not prey on anything that is dead or sleeping. Then Orlando looked at the man, and saw that it was his wicked brother, Oliver, who had tried to take his life. He fought with the lioness and killed her, and saved his brother's life.

While Orlando was fighting the lioness, Oliver woke to see his brother, whom he had treated so badly, saving him from a wild beast at the risk of his own life. This made him repent of his wickedness, and he begged Orlando's pardon, and from thenceforth they were dear brothers. The lioness had wounded Orlando's arm so much, that he could not go on to see the shepherd, so he sent his brother to ask Ganymede to come to him.

Oliver went and told the whole story to Ganymede and Aliena, and Aliena was so charmed with his manly way of confessing his faults, that she fell in love with him at once. But when Ganymede heard of the danger Orlando had been in she fainted; and when she came to herself, said truly enough, "I should have been a woman by right."

Oliver went back to his brother and told him all this, saying, "I love Aliena so well that I will give up my estates to you and marry her, and live here as a shepherd."

"Let your wedding be to-morrow," said Orlando, "and I will ask the Duke and his friends."

When Orlando told Ganymede how his brother was to be married on the morrow, he added: "Oh, how bitter a thing it is to look into happiness through another man's eyes."

Then answered Rosalind, still in Ganymede's dress and speaking with his voice—"If you do love Rosalind so near the heart, then when your brother marries Aliena, shall you marry her."

Now the next day the Duke and his followers, and Orlando, and Oliver, and Aliena, were all gathered together for the wedding.

Then Ganymede came in and said to the Duke, "If I bring in your daughter Rosalind, will you give her to Orlando here?" "That I would," said the Duke, "if I had all kingdoms to give with her."

"And you say you will have her when I bring her?" she said to Orlando. "That would I," he answered, "were I king of all kingdoms."

Then Rosalind and Celia went out, and Rosalind put on her pretty woman's clothes again, and after a while came back.

She turned to her father—"I give myself to you, for I am yours." "If there be truth in sight," he said, "you are my daughter."

Then she said to Orlando, "I give myself to you, for I am yours." "If there be truth in sight," he said, "you are my Rosalind."

"I will have no father if you be not he," she said to the Duke, and to Orlando, "I will have no husband if you be not he."

So Orlando and Rosalind were married, and Oliver and Celia, and they lived happy ever after, returning with the Duke to the kingdom. For Frederick had been shown by a holy hermit the wickedness of his ways, and so gave back the duke-dom of his brother, and himself went into a monastery to pray for forgiveness.

The wedding was a merry one, in the mossy glades of the forest. A shepherd and shepherdess who had been friends with Rosalind, when she was herself disguised as a shepherd, were married on the same day, and all with such pretty feastings and merrymakings as could be nowhere within four walls, but only in the beautiful green wood.

Hamlet

Illustrations by Harold Copping, c. 1900

Hamlet was the only son of the King of Denmark. He loved his father and mother dearly--and was happy in the love of a sweet lady named Ophelia. Her father, Polonius, was the King's Chamberlain, the officer in charge of his castle.

While Hamlet was away studying at Wittenberg, his father died. Young Hamlet hastened home in great grief to hear that a serpent had stung the King, and that he was dead. The young Prince had loved his father so tenderly that you may judge what he felt when he found that the Queen, before yet the King had been laid in the ground a month, had determined to marry again--and to marry the dead King's brother.

Hamlet refused to put off mourning for the wedding.

"It is not only the black I wear on my body," he said, "that proves my loss. I wear mourning in my heart for my dead father. His son at least remembers him, and grieves still."

Then said Claudius the King's brother, "This grief is unreasonable. Of course you must sorrow at the loss of your father, but--"

"Ah," said Hamlet, bitterly, "I cannot in one little month forget those I love."

With that the Queen and Claudius left him, to make merry over their wedding, forgetting the poor good King who had been so kind to them both.

And Hamlet, left alone, began to wonder and to question as to what he ought to do. For he could not believe the story about the snake-bite. It seemed to him all too plain that the wicked Claudius had killed the King, so as to get the crown and marry the Queen. Yet he had no proof, and could not accuse Claudius.

And while he was thus thinking came Horatio, a fellow student of his, from Wittenberg.

"What brought you here?" asked Hamlet, when he had greeted his friend kindly.

"I came, my lord, to see your father's funeral."

"I think it was to see my mother's wedding," said Hamlet, bitterly. "My father! We shall not look upon his like again."

"My lord," answered Horatio, "I think I saw him yesternight."

Then, while Hamlet listened in surprise, Horatio told how he, with two gentlemen of the guard, had seen the King's ghost on the battlements. Hamlet went that night, and true enough, at midnight, the ghost of the King, in the armor he had been wont to wear, appeared on the battlements in the chill moonlight. Hamlet was a brave youth. Instead of running away from the ghost he spoke to it--and when it beckoned him he followed it to a quiet place, and there the ghost told him that what he had suspected was true. The wicked Claudius had indeed killed his good brother the King, by dropping poison into his ear as he slept in his orchard in the afternoon.

"And you," said the ghost, "must avenge this cruel murder-- on my wicked brother. But do nothing against the Queen– for I have loved her, and she is your mother. Remember me."

Then seeing the morning approach, the ghost vanished.

"Now," said Hamlet, "there is nothing left but revenge. Remember thee--I will remember nothing else--books, pleasure, youth--let all go--and your commands alone live on my brain."

So when his friends came back, he made them swear to keep the secret of the ghost, and then went in from the battlements, now gray with mingled dawn and moonlight, to think how he might best avenge his murdered father.

The shock of seeing and hearing his father's ghost made him feel almost mad, and for fear that his uncle might notice that he was not himself, he determined to hide his mad longing for revenge under a pretended madness in other matters.

And when he met Ophelia, who loved him--and to whom he had given gifts, and letters, and many loving words--he behaved so wildly to her, that she could not but think him mad. For she loved him so that she could not believe he would be as cruel as this, unless he were quite mad. So she told her father, and showed him a pretty letter from Hamlet. And in the letter was much folly, and this pretty verse--

"Doubt that the stars are fire; Doubt that the sun doth move; Doubt truth to be a liar;

But never doubt I love."

And from that time everyone believed that the cause of Hamlet's supposed madness was love.

Poor Hamlet was very unhappy. He longed to obey his father's ghost--and yet he was too gentle and kindly to wish to kill another man, even his father's murderer. And sometimes he wondered whether, after all, the ghost spoke truly.

Just at this time some actors came to the Court, and Hamlet ordered them to perform a certain play before the King and Queen. Now, this play was the story of a man who had been murdered in his garden by a near relation, who afterwards married the dead man's wife.

You may imagine the feelings of the wicked King, as he sat on his throne, with the Queen beside him and all his Court around, and saw, acted on the stage, the very wickedness that he had himself done. And when, in the play, the wicked relation poured poison into the ear of the sleeping man, the wicked Claudius suddenly rose, and staggered from the room--the Queen and others following.

Then said Hamlet to his friends--

"Now I am sure the ghost spoke true. For if Claudius had not done this murder, he could not have been so distressed to see it in a play."

Now the Queen sent for Hamlet, by the King's desire, to scold him for his conduct during the play, and for other matters; and Claudius, wishing to know exactly what happened, told old Polonius to hide himself behind the hangings in the Queen's room. And as they talked, the Queen got frightened at Hamlet's rough, strange words, and cried for help, and Polonius behind the curtain cried out too. Hamlet, thinking it was the King who was hidden there, thrust with his sword at the hangings, and killed, not the King, but poor old Polonius.

So now Hamlet had offended his uncle and his mother, and by bad happenstance killed his true love's father.

"Oh! what a rash and bloody deed is this," cried the Queen.

And Hamlet answered bitterly, "Almost as bad as to kill a king, and marry his brother." Then Hamlet told the Queen plainly all his thoughts and how he knew of the murder, and begged

her, at least, to have no more friendship or kindness of the base Claudius, who had killed the good King. And as they spoke the King's ghost again appeared before Hamlet, but the Queen could not see it. So when the ghost had gone, they parted.

When the Queen told Claudius what had passed, and how Polonius was dead, he said, "This shows plainly that Hamlet is mad, and since he has killed Polonius, it is for his own safety that we must carry out our plan, and send him away to England."

So Hamlet was sent, under charge of two courtiers who served the King, and these bore letters to the English Court, requiring that Hamlet should be put to death. But Hamlet had the good sense to get at these letters, and put in others instead, with the names of the two courtiers who were so ready to betray him. Then, as the vessel went to England, Hamlet escaped on board a pirate ship, and the two wicked courtiers left him to his fate, and went on to meet theirs.

Hamlet hurried home, but in the meantime a dreadful thing had happened. Poor pretty Ophelia, having lost her lover and her father, lost her wits too, and went in sad madness about the Court, with straws, and weeds, and flowers in her hair, singing strange scraps of songs, and talking poor, foolish, pretty talk with no heart of meaning to it. And one day, coming to a stream where willows grew, she tried to hang a flowery garland on a willow, and fell into the water with all her flowers, and so died.

And Hamlet had loved her, though his plan of seeming madness had made him hide it; and when he came back, he found the King and Queen, and the Court, weeping at the funeral of his dear love and lady.

Ophelia's brother, Laertes, had also just come to Court to ask justice for the death of his father, old Polonius; and now, wild with grief, he leaped into his sister's grave, to clasp her in his arms once more.

"I loved her more than forty thousand brothers," cried Hamlet, and leapt into the grave after him, and they fought till they were parted.

Afterwards Hamlet begged Laertes to forgive him.

"I could not bear," he said, "that any, even a brother, should seem to love her more than I."

But the wicked Claudius would not let them be friends. He told Laertes how Hamlet had killed old Polonius, and between them they made a plot to slay Hamlet by treachery.

Laertes challenged him to a fencing match, and all the Court were present. Hamlet had the blunt foil always used in fencing, but Laertes had prepared for himself a sword, sharp, and tipped with poison. And the wicked King had made ready a bowl of poisoned wine, which he meant to give poor Hamlet when he should grow warm with the sword play, and should call for drink.

So Laertes and Hamlet fought, and Laertes, after some fencing, gave Hamlet a sharp sword thrust. Hamlet, angry at this treachery--for they had been fencing, not as men fight, but as they play--closed with Laertes in a struggle; both dropped their swords, and when they picked them up again, Hamlet, without noticing it, had exchanged his own blunt sword for Laertes' sharp and poisoned one. And with one thrust of it he pierced Laertes, who fell dead by his own treachery.

At this moment the Queen cried out, "The drink, the drink! Oh, my dear Hamlet! I am poisoned!"

She had drunk of the poisoned bowl the King had prepared for Hamlet, and the King saw the Queen, whom, wicked as he was, he really loved, fall dead by his means.

Then Ophelia being dead, and Polonius, and the Queen, and Laertes, and the two courtiers who had been sent to England, Hamlet at last found courage to do the ghost's bidding and avenge his father's murder--which, if he had braced up his heart to do long before, all these lives had been spared, and none had suffered but the wicked King, who well deserved to die.

Hamlet, his heart at last being great enough to do the deed he ought, turned the poisoned sword on the false King.

"Then--venom--do thy work!" he cried, and the King died.

So Hamlet in the end kept the promise he had made his father. And all being now accomplished, he himself died. And those who stood by saw him die, with prayers and tears, for his friends and his people loved him with their whole hearts. Thus ends the tragic tale of Hamlet, Prince of Denmark.

The Comedy of Errors

Illustrations by Louis Rhead, 1918

Aegeon was a merchant of Syracuse, which is a seaport in Sicily. His wife was Aemilia, and they were very happy until Aegeon's manager died, and he was obliged to go by himself to a place called Epidamnum on the Adriatic. As soon as she could Aemilia followed him, and after they had been together some time two baby boys were born to them. The babies were exactly alike; even when they were dressed differently they looked the same.

And now you must believe a very strange thing. At the same inn where these children were born, and on the same day, two baby boys were born to a much poorer couple than Aemilia and Aegeon; so poor, indeed, were the parents of these twins that they sold them to the parents of the other twins as servants.

Aemilia was eager to show her children to her friends in Syracuse, and in treacherous weather she and Aegeon and the four babies sailed homewards.

They were still far from Syracuse when their ship sprang a leak, and the crew left in the only boat, caring little what became of their passengers.

Aemilia fastened one of her children to a mast and tied one of the servant-children to him; Aegeon followed her example with the remaining children. Then the parents secured themselves to the same masts, and hoped for safety.

The ship, however, suddenly struck a rock and was split in two, and Aemilia, and the two children whom she had tied, floated away from Aegeon and the other children. Aemilia and her charges were picked up by some people of Epidamnum, but some fishermen of Corinth took the babies from her by force, and she returned to Epidanmum alone, and very miserable. Afterwards she settled in Ephesus, a famous town in Asia Minor.

Aegeon and his charges were also saved; and, more fortunate than Aemilia, he was able to return to Syracuse and keep them till they were eighteen. His own child he called Antipholus, and the servant child he called Dromio; and, strangely enough, these were the names given to the children who floated away from him.

At the age of eighteen the son who was with Aegeon grew restless with a desire to find his brother. Aegeon let him depart with his servant, and the young men are henceforth known as Antipholus of Syracuse and Dromio of Syracuse.

Let alone, Aegeon found his home too dreary to dwell in, and traveled for five years. He did not, during his absence, learn all the news of Syracuse, or he would never have gone to Ephesus.

As it was, his melancholy wandering ceased in that town, where he was arrested almost as soon as he arrived. He then found that the Duke of Syracuse had been acting in so tyrannical a manner to Ephesians unlucky enough to fall into his hands, that the Government of Ephesus had angrily passed a law which punished by death or a fine of a thousand pounds any Syracusan who should come to Ephesus. Aegeon was brought before Solinus, Duke of Ephesus, who told him that he must die or pay a thousand pounds before the end of the day.

You will think there was fate in this when I tell you that the children who were kidnaped by the fishermen of Corinth were now citizens of Ephesus, whither they had been brought by Duke Menaphon, an uncle of Duke Solinus. They will henceforth be called Antipholus of Ephesus and Dromio of Ephesus.

Moreover, on the very day when Aegeon was arrested, Antipholus of Syracuse landed in Ephesus and pretended that he came from Epidamnum in order to avoid a penalty. He handed his money to his servant Dromio of Syracuse, and bade him take it to the Centaur Inn and remain there till he came.

In less than ten minutes he was met on the Mart by Dromio of Ephesus, his brother's servant, and immediately mistook him for his own Dromio. "Why are you back so soon? Where did you leave the money?" asked Antipholus of Syracuse.

This Dromio knew of no money except sixpence, which he had received on the previous Wednesday and given to the saddler; but he did know that his mistress was annoyed because his master was not in to dinner, and he asked Antipholus of Syracuse to go to a house called The Phoenix without delay. His speech angered the hearer, and Dromio fled. Antipholus of Syracuse then went to The Centaur, found that his gold had been deposited

there, and walked out of the inn.

He was wandering about Ephesus when two beautiful ladies signaled to him with their hands. They were sisters, and their names were Adriana and Luciana. Adriana was the wife of his brother Antipholus of Ephesus, and she had made up her mind, from the strange account given her by Dromio of Ephesus, that her husband preferred another woman to his wife. "Ay, you may look as if you did not know me," she said to the man who was really her brother-in-law, "but I can remember when no words were sweet unless I said them, no meat flavorsome unless I carved it."

"Is it I you address?" said Antipholus of Syracuse stiffly. "I do not know you."

"Fie, brother," said Luciana. "You know perfectly well that she sent Dromio to you to bid you come to dinner;" and Adriana said, "Come, come; I have been made a fool of long enough. My truant husband shall dine with me and confess his silly pranks and be forgiven."

They were determined ladies, and Antipholus of Syracuse grew weary of disputing with them, and followed them obediently to The Phoenix, where a very late "mid-day" dinner awaited them.

They were at dinner when Antipholus of Ephesus and his slave Dromio demanded admittance. "Maud, Bridget, Marian, Cecily, Gillian, Ginn!" shouted Dromio of Ephesus, who knew all his fellow-servants' names by heart.

From within came the reply, "Fool, dray-horse, coxcomb, idiot!" It was Dromio of Syracuse unconsciously insulting his brother.

Master and man did their best to get in, short of using a crowbar, and finally went away; but Antipholus of Ephesus felt so annoyed with his wife that he decided to give a gold chain which he had promised her, to another woman.

Inside The Phoenix, Luciana, who believed Antipholus of Syracuse to be her sister's husband, attempted, by a discourse in rhyme, when alone with him, to make him kinder to Adriana. In reply he told her that he was not married, but that he loved her so much that, if Luciana were a mermaid, he would gladly lie on the sea if he might feel beneath him her floating golden hair.

Luciana was shocked and left him, and reported his lovemaking to Adriana, who said that her husband was old and ugly, and not fit to be seen or heard, though secretly she was very fond of him.

Antipholus of Syracuse soon received a visitor in the shape of Angelo the goldsmith, of whom Antipholus of Ephesus had ordered the chain which he had promised his wife and intended to give to another woman.

The goldsmith handed the chain to Antipholus of Syracuse, and treated his "I bespoke it not" as mere fun, so that the puzzled merchant took the chain as good-humoredly as he had partaken of Adriana's dinner. He offered payment, but Angelo foolishly said he would call again.

The consequence was that Angelo was without money when a creditor of the sort that stands no nonsense, threatened him with arrest unless he paid his debt immediately. This creditor had brought a police officer with him, and Angelo was relieved to see Antipholus of Ephesus coming out of the house where he had been dining because he been locked out of The Phoenix. Bitter was Angelo's dismay when Antipholus denied receipt of the chain. Angelo could have sent his mother to prison if she had said that, and he gave Antipholus of Ephesus in charge, to be sent to jail.

At this moment up came Dromio of Syracuse and told the wrong Antipholus that he had shipped his goods, and that a favorable wind was blowing. To the ears of Antipholus of Ephesus this talk was simple nonsense. He crossly told him to hurry to Adriana and bid her send to her arrested husband a purse of money which she would find in his desk.

Though Adriana was furious with her husband because she thought he had been making love to her sister, she did not prevent Luciana from getting the purse, and she bade Dromio of Syracuse bring home his master immediately.

Unfortunately, before Dromio could reach the police station he met his real master, who had never been arrested, and did not understand what he meant by offering him a purse. Antipholus of Syracuse was further surprised when a lady whom he did not know asked him for a chain that he had promised her. She was, of course, the lady with whom Antipholus of Ephesus had dined when his brother was occupying his place at table. "Avaunt, thou witch!" was the answer which, to her astonishment, she received.

Meanwhile Antipholus of Ephesus waited vainly for the money which was to have released him. Never a good-tempered man, he was crazy with anger when Dromio of Ephesus, who, of course, had not been instructed to fetch a purse, appeared with nothing more useful than a rope. And his temper did not mend when Adriana, Luciana, and a doctor arrived under the impression that he was mad. He raged so much that men came forward to bind him. But the kindness of Adriana spared him this shame. She promised to pay the sum demanded of him, and asked the doctor to lead him to The Phoenix.

Angelo's merchant creditor being paid, the two were friendly again, and might soon have been seen chatting before an abbey about the odd behavior of Antipholus of Ephesus. "Softly," said the merchant at last, "that's he, I think."

It was not; it was Antipholus of Syracuse with his servant Dromio, and he wore Angelo's chain round his neck! The reconciled pair fairly pounced upon him to know what he meant by denying the receipt of the chain he had the impudence to wear. Antipholus of Syracuse lost his temper, and drew his sword, and at that moment Adriana and several others appeared. "Hold!" shouted the careful wife. "Hurt him not; he is mad. Take his sword away. Bind him--and Dromio too."

Dromio of Syracuse did not wish to be bound, and he said to his master, "Run, master! Into that abbey, quick, or we shall be robbed!"

They accordingly retreated into the abbey.

Adriana, Luciana, and a crowd remained outside, and the Abbess came out, and said, "People, why do you gather here?"

"To fetch my poor distracted husband," replied Adriana.

Angelo and the merchant remarked that they had not known that he was mad.

Adriana then told the Abbess rather too much about her wifely worries, for the Abbess received the idea that Adriana was a shrew, and that if her husband was distracted he had better not return to her for the present.

Adriana determined, therefore, to complain to Duke Solinus, and, lo and behold! a minute afterwards the great man appeared with officers and two others. The others were Aegeon and the headsman. The thousand marks had not been found, and Aegeon's fate seemed sealed.

Ere the Duke could pass the abbey Adriana knelt before him, and told a woeful tale of a mad husband rushing about stealing jewelry and drawing his sword, adding that the Abbess refused to allow her to lead him home.

The Duke bade the Abbess be summoned, and no sooner had he given the order than a servant from The Phoenix ran to Adriana with the tale that his master had singed off the doctor's beard.

"Nonsense!" said Adriana, "he's in the abbey."

"As sure as I live I speak the truth," said the servant.

Antipholus of Syracuse had not come out of the abbey, before his brother of Ephesus prostrated himself in front of the Duke, exclaiming, "Justice, most gracious Duke, against that woman." He pointed to Adriana. "She has treated another man like her husband in my own house."

Even while he was speaking Aegeon said, "Unless I am delirious, I see my son Antipholus."

No one noticed him, and Antipholus of Ephesus went on to say how the doctor, whom he called "a threadbare juggler," had been one of a gang who tied him to his servant Dromio, and thrust them into a vault whence he had escaped by gnawing through his bonds.

The Duke could not understand how the same man who spoke to him was seen to go into the abbey, and he was still wondering when Aegeon asked Antipholus of Ephesus if he was not his son. He replied, "I never saw my father in my life;" but so deceived was Aegeon by his likeness to the brother whom he had brought up, that he said, "Thou art ashamed to acknowledge me in misery."

Soon, however, the Abbess advanced with Antipholus of Syracuse and Dromio of Syracuse.

Then cried Adriana, "I see two husbands or mine eyes deceive me;" and Antipholus, espying his father, said, "Thou art Aegeon or his ghost."

It was a day of surprises, for the Abbess said, "I will free that man by paying his fine, and gain my husband whom I lost. Speak, Aegeon, for I am thy wife Aemilia."

The Duke was touched. "He is free without a fine," he said.

So Aegeon and Aemilia were reunited, and Adriana and her husband reconciled; but no one was happier than Antipholus of Syracuse, who, in the Duke's presence, went to Luciana and said, "I told you I loved you. Will you be my wife?"

Her answer was given by a look, and therefore is not written.

The two Dromios were glad to think they would receive no more trouble.

Twelfth Night

Illustrations by W. Heath Robinson, 1908

Orsino, the Duke of Illyria, was deeply in love with a beautiful Countess named Olivia. Yet all his love was in vain, for she disdained his suit; and when her brother died, she sent back a messenger from the Duke, bidding him tell his master that for seven years she would not let the very air behold her face, but that, like a nun, she would walk veiled; and all this for the sake of a dead brother's love, which she would keep fresh and lasting in her sad remembrance.

The Duke longed for someone to whom he could tell his sorrow, and repeat over and over again the story of his love. And chance brought him such a companion. For about this time a goodly ship was wrecked on the Illyrian coast, and among those who reached land in safety were the captain and a fair young maid, named Viola. But she was little grateful for being rescued from the perils of the sea, since she feared that her twin brother was drowned, Sebastian, as dear to her as the heart in her bosom, and so like her that, but for the difference in their manner of dress, one could hardly be told from the other. The captain, for her comfort, told her that he had seen her brother bind himself "to a strong mast that lived upon the sea," and that thus there was hope that he might be saved.

Viola now asked in whose country she was, and learning that the young Duke Orsino ruled there, and was as noble in his nature as in his name, she decided to disguise herself in male attire, and seek for employment with him as a page.

In this she succeeded, and now from day to day she had to listen to the story of Orsino's love. At first she sympathized very truly with him, but soon her sympathy grew to love. At last it occurred to Orsino that his hopeless love-suit might prosper better if he sent this pretty lad to woo Olivia for him. Viola unwillingly went on this errand, but when she came to the house, Malvolio, Olivia's steward, a vain, officious man, sick, as his mistress told him, of self-love, forbade the messenger admittance.

Viola, however (who was now called Cesario), refused to take any denial, and vowed to have speech with the Countess. Olivia, hearing how her instructions were defied and

curious to see this daring youth, said, "We'll once more hear Orsino's embassy."

When Viola was admitted to her presence and the servants had been sent away, she listened patiently to the reproaches which this bold messenger from the Duke poured upon her, and listening she fell in love with the supposed Cesario; and when Cesario had gone, Olivia longed to send some love-token after him. So, calling Malvolio, she bade him follow the boy.

"He left this ring behind him," she said, taking one from her finger. "Tell him I will have none of it."

Malvolio did as he was bid, and then Viola, who of course knew perfectly well that she had left no ring behind her, saw with a woman's quickness that Olivia loved her. Then she went back to the Duke, very sad at heart for her lover, and for Olivia, and for herself.

It was but cold comfort she could give Orsino, who now sought to ease the pangs of despised love by listening to sweet music, while Cesario stood by his side.

"Ah," said the Duke to his page that night, "you too have been in love."

"A little," answered Viola.

"What kind of woman is it?" he asked.

"Of your complexion," she answered.

"What years?" was his next question.

To this came the pretty answer, "About your years, my lord."

"Too old, by Heaven!" cried the Duke. "Let still the woman take an elder than herself."

And Viola very meekly said, "I think it well, my lord."

By and by Orsino begged Cesario once more to visit Olivia and to plead his love-suit. But she, thinking to dissuade him, said--

"If some lady loved you as you love Olivia?"

"Ah! that cannot be," said the Duke.

"But I know," Viola went on, "what love woman may have for a man. My father had a daughter loved a man, as it might be," she added blushing, "perhaps, were I a woman, I should love your lordship."

"And what is her history?" he asked.

"A blank, my lord," Viola answered. "She never told her love, but let concealment like a worm in the bud feed on her damask cheek: she pined in thought, and with a green and yellow melancholy she sat, like Patience on a monument, smiling at grief. Was not this love indeed?"

"But died thy sister of her love, my boy?" the Duke asked; and Viola, who had all the time been telling her own love for him in this pretty fashion, said--

"I am all the daughters my father has and all the brothers— Sir, shall I go to the lady?"

"To her in haste," said the Duke, at once forgetting all about the story, "and give her this jewel."

So Viola went, and this time poor Olivia was unable to hide her love, and openly confessed it with such passionate truth, that Viola left her hastily, saying--

"Nevermore will I deplore my master's tears to you."

But in vowing this, Viola did not know the tender pity she would feel for other's suffering. So when Olivia, in the violence of her love, sent a messenger, praying Cesario to visit her once more, Cesario had no heart to refuse the request.

But the favors which Olivia bestowed upon this mere page aroused the jealousy of Sir Andrew Aguecheek, a foolish, rejected lover of hers, who at that time was staying at her house with her merry old uncle Sir Toby. This same Sir Toby dearly loved a practical joke, and knowing Sir Andrew to be an arrant coward, he thought that if he could bring off a duel between him and Cesario, there would be rare entertainment indeed. So he induced Sir Andrew to send a challenge, which he himself took to Cesario. The poor page, in great terror, said--

"I will return again to the house, I am no fighter."

"Back you shall not to the house," said Sir Toby, "unless you fight me first."

W·HEATH·ROBINSON

And as he looked a very fierce old gentleman, Viola thought it best to await Sir Andrew's coming; and when he at last made his appearance, in a great fright, if the truth had been known, she tremblingly drew her sword, and Sir Andrew in like fear followed her example. Happily for them both, at this moment some officers of the Court came on the scene, and stopped the intended duel. Viola gladly made off with what speed she might, while Sir Toby called after her--

"A very paltry boy, and more a coward than a hare!"

Now, while these things were happening, Sebastian had escaped all the dangers of the deep, and had landed safely in Illyria, where he determined to make his way to the Duke's Court. On his way thither he passed Olivia's house just as Viola had left it in such a hurry, and whom should he meet but Sir Andrew and Sir Toby. Sir Andrew, mistaking Sebastian for the cowardly Cesario, took his courage in both hands, and walking up to him struck him, saying, "There's for you."

"Why, there's for you; and there, and there!" said Sebastian, hitting back a great deal harder, and again, till Sir Toby came to the rescue of his friend. Sebastian, however, tore himself free from Sir Toby's clutches, and drawing his sword would have fought them both, but that Olivia herself, having heard of the quarrel, came running in, and with many reproaches sent Sir Toby and his friend away. Then turning to Sebastian, whom she too thought to be Cesario, she besought him with many a pretty speech to come into the house with her.

Sebastian, half dazed and all delighted with her beauty and grace, readily consented, and that very day, so great was Olivia's haste, they were married before she had discovered that he was not Cesario, or Sebastian was quite certain whether or not he was in a dream.

Meanwhile Orsino, hearing how poorly Cesario fared with Olivia, visited her himself, taking Cesario with him. Olivia met them both before her door, and seeing, as she thought, her husband there, reproached him for leaving her, while to the Duke she said that his suit was as fat and wholesome to her as howling after music.

"Still so cruel?" said Orsino.

"Still so constant," she answered.

Then Orsino's anger growing to cruelty, he vowed that, to be revenged on her, he would kill Cesario, whom he knew she loved. "Come, boy," he said to the page.

And Viola, following him as he moved away, said, "I, to do you rest, a thousand deaths would die."

A great fear took hold on Olivia, and she cried aloud, "Cesario, husband, stay!"

"Her husband?" asked the Duke angrily.

"No, my lord, not I," said Viola.

"Call forth the holy father," cried Olivia.

And the priest who had married Sebastian and Olivia, coming in, declared Cesario to be the bridegroom.

"O thou dissembling cub!" the Duke exclaimed. "Farewell, and take her, but go where thou and I henceforth may never meet."

At this moment Sir Andrew came up with bleeding crown, complaining that Cesario had broken his head, and Sir Toby's as well.

"I never hurt you," said Viola, very positively; "you drew your sword on me, but I bespoke you fair, and hurt you not."

Yet, for all her protesting, no one there believed her; but all their thoughts were on a sudden changed to wonder, when Sebastian came in.

"I am sorry, madam," he said to his wife, "I have hurt your kinsman. Pardon me, sweet, even for the vows we made each other so late ago."

"One face, one voice, one habit, and two persons!" cried the Duke, looking first at Viola, and then at Sebastian.

"An apple cleft in two," said one who knew Sebastian, "is not more twin than these two creatures. Which is Sebastian?"

"I never had a brother," said Sebastian. "I had a sister, whom the blind waves and surges have devoured." "Were you a woman," he said to Viola, "I should let my tears fall upon your cheek, and say, 'Thrice welcome, drowned Viola!'"

Then Viola, rejoicing to see her dear brother alive, confessed that she was indeed his sister, Viola. As she spoke, Orsino felt the pity that is akin to love.

"Boy," he said, "thou hast said to me a thousand times thou never shouldst love woman like to me."

"And all those sayings will I overswear," Viola replied, "and all those swearings keep true."

"Give me thy hand," Orsino cried in gladness. "Thou shalt be my wife, and my fancy's queen."

Thus was the gentle Viola made happy, while Olivia found in Sebastian a constant lover, and a good husband, and he in her a true and loving wife.

Tempest

Illustrations by Edmund Dulac, 1908

Prospero, the Duke of Milan, was a learned and studious man, who lived among his books, leaving the management of his dukedom to his brother Antonio, in whom indeed he had complete trust. But that trust was ill-rewarded, for Antonio wanted to wear the duke's crown himself, and, to gain his ends, would have killed his brother but for the love the people bore him. However, with the help of Prospero's great enemy, Alonso, King of Naples, he managed to get into his hands the dukedom with all its honor, power, and riches. For they took Prospero to sea, and when they were far away from land, forced him into a little boat with no tackle, mast, or sail. In their cruelty and hatred they put his little daughter, Miranda (not yet three years old), into the boat with him, and sailed away, leaving them to their fate.

But one among the courtiers with Antonio was true to his rightful master, Prospero. To save the duke from his enemies was impossible, but much could be done to remind him of a subject's love. So this worthy lord, whose name was Gonzalo, secretly placed in the boat some fresh water, provisions, and clothes, and what Prospero valued most of all, some of his precious books.

The boat was cast on an island, and Prospero and his little one landed in safety. Now this island was enchanted, and for years had lain under the spell of a fell witch, Sycorax, who had imprisoned in the trunks of trees all the good spirits she found there. She died shortly before Prospero was cast on those shores, but the spirits, of whom Ariel was the chief, still remained in their prisons.

Prospero was a great magician, for he had devoted himself almost entirely to the study of magic during the years in which he allowed his brother to manage the affairs of Milan. By his art he set free the imprisoned spirits, yet kept them obedient to his will, and they were more truly his subjects than his people in Milan had been. For he treated them kindly as long as they did his bidding, and he exercised his power over them wisely and well. One creature alone he found it necessary to treat with harshness: this was Caliban, the son of

the wicked old witch, a hideous, deformed monster, horrible to look on, and vicious and brutal in all his habits.

When Miranda was grown up into a maiden, sweet and fair to see, it chanced that Antonio and Alonso, with Sebastian, his brother, and Ferdinand, his son, were at sea together with old Gonzalo, and their ship came near Prospero's island. Prospero, knowing they were there, raised by his art a great storm, so that even the sailors on board gave themselves up for lost; and first among them all Prince Ferdinand leaped into the sea, and, as his father Alonso thought in his grief, was drowned. But Ariel brought him safe ashore; and all the rest of the crew, although they were washed overboard, were landed unhurt in different parts of the island, and the good ship herself, which they all thought had been wrecked, lay at anchor in the harbor whither Ariel had brought her. Such wonders could Prospero and his spirits perform.

While yet the tempest was raging, Prospero showed his daughter the brave ship laboring in the trough of the sea, and told her that it was filled with living human beings like themselves. She, in pity of their lives, prayed him who had raised this storm to quell it. Then her father bade her to have no fear, for he intended to save every one of them.

Then, for the first time, he told her the story of his life and hers, and that he had caused this storm to rise in order that his enemies, his brother Antonio and Alonso, King of Naples, who were on board, might be delivered into his hands.

When he had made an end of his story he charmed her into sleep, for Ariel was at hand, and he had work for him to do. Ariel, who longed for his complete freedom, grumbled to be kept in drudgery, but on being reminded of all the sufferings he had undergone when Sycorax ruled in the land, and of the debt of gratitude he owed to the master who had made those sufferings to end, he ceased to complain, and promised faithfully to do whatever Prospero might command.

"Do so," said Prospero, "and in two days I will discharge thee."

Then he bade Ariel take the form of a water nymph and sent him in search of the young prince. And Ariel, invisible to Ferdinand, hovered near him, singing the while--

"Come unto these yellow sands And then take hands: Court'sied when you have, and kiss'd (The wild waves whist), Foot it featly here and there; And, sweet sprites, the burden bear!"

And Ferdinand followed the magic singing, as the song changed to a solemn air, and the words brought grief to his heart, and tears to his eyes, for thus they ran--

"Full fathom five thy father lies; Of his bones are coral made. Those are pearls that were his eyes, Nothing of him that doth fade, But doth suffer a sea-change Into something rich and strange. Sea-nymphs hourly ring his knell. Hark! now I hear them,-- ding dong bell!"

And so singing, Ariel led the spell-bound prince into the presence of Prospero and Miranda. Then, behold! all happened as Prospero desired. For Miranda, who had never, since she could first remember, seen any human being save her father, looked on the youthful prince with reverence in her eyes, and love in her secret heart.

"I might call him," she said, "a thing divine, for nothing natural I ever saw so noble!"

And Ferdinand, beholding her beauty with wonder and delight, exclaimed--

"Most sure the goddess on whom these airs attend!"

Nor did he attempt to hide the passion which she inspired in him, for scarcely had they exchanged half a dozen sentences, before he vowed to make her his queen if she were willing. But Prospero, though secretly delighted, pretended wrath.

"You come here as a spy," he said to Ferdinand. "I will manacle your neck and feet together, and you shall feed on fresh water mussels, withered roots and husk, and have sea-water to drink. Follow."

"No," said Ferdinand, and drew his sword. But on the instant Prospero charmed him so that he stood there like a statue, still as stone; and Miranda in terror prayed her father to have mercy on her lover. But he harshly refused her, and made Ferdinand follow him to his cell. There he set the Prince to work, making him remove thousands of heavy logs of timber and pile them up; and Ferdinand patiently obeyed, and thought his toil all too well repaid by the sympathy of the sweet Miranda.

She in very pity would have helped him in his hard work, but he would not let her, yet he could not keep from her the secret of his love, and she, hearing it, rejoiced and promised to be his wife.

Then Prospero released him from his servitude, and glad at heart, he gave his consent to their marriage.

"Take her," he said, "she is thine own."

In the meantime, Antonio and Sebastian in another part of the island were plotting the murder of Alonso, the King of Naples, for Ferdinand being dead, as they thought, his brother Sebastian would succeed to the throne on Alonso's death. And they would have carried out their wicked purpose while their victim was asleep, but that Ariel woke him in good time.

Many tricks did Ariel play them. Once he set a banquet before them, and just as they were going to fall to, he appeared to them amid thunder and lightning in the form of a harpy, and immediately the banquet disappeared. Then Ariel upbraided them with their sins and vanished too.

Prospero by his enchantments drew them all to the grove without his cell, where they waited, trembling and afraid, and now at last bitterly repenting them of their sins.

Prospero determined to make one last use of his magic power, "And then," said he, "I'll break my staff and deeper than did ever plummet sound I'll drown my book."

So he made heavenly music to sound in the air, and appeared to them in his proper shape as the Duke of Milan. Because they repented, he forgave them and told them the story of his life since they had cruelly committed him and his baby daughter to the mercy of wind and waves. Alonso King of Naples, who seemed sorriest of them all for his past crimes, lamented the loss of his heir. But Prospero drew back a curtain and showed them Ferdinand and Miranda playing at chess. Great was Alonso's joy to greet his loved son again, and when he heard that the fair maid with whom Ferdinand was playing was Prospero's daughter, and that the young folks had plighted their troth, he said--

"Give me your hands, let grief and sorrow still embrace his heart that doth not wish you joy."

So all ended happily. The ship was safe in the harbor, and next day they all set sail for Naples, where Ferdinand and Miranda were to be married. Ariel gave them calm seas and auspicious gales; and many were the rejoicings at the wedding.

Then Prospero, after many years of absence, went back to his own dukedom, where he was welcomed with great joy by his faithful subjects. He practiced the arts of magic no more, but his life was happy, and not only because he had found his own again, but chiefly because, when his bitterest foes who had done him deadly wrong lay at his mercy, he took no vengeance on them, but nobly forgave them.

As for Ariel, Prospero made him free as air, so that he could wander where he would, and sing with a light heart his sweet song--

"Where the bee sucks, there suck I: In a cowslip's bell I lie; There I couch when owls do cry. On the bat's back I do fly After summer, merrily: Merrily, merrily, shall I live now, Under the blossom that hangs on the bough."

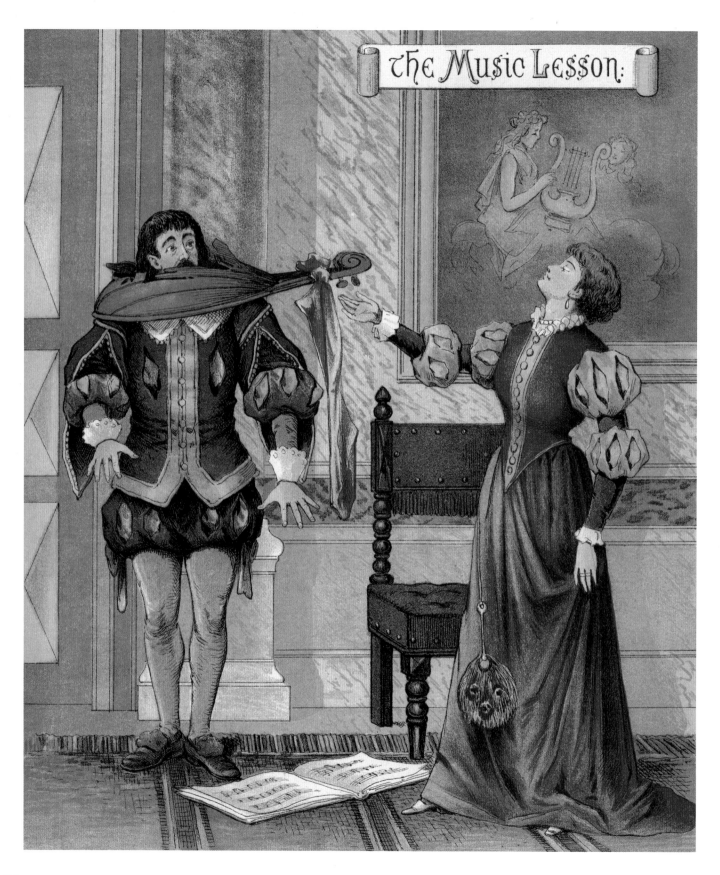

Taming Of The Shrew

Illustrations by R. André, 1881

There lived in Padua a gentleman named Baptista, who had two fair daughters. The eldest, Katharine, was so very cross and ill-tempered, and unmannerly, that no one ever dreamed of marrying her, while her sister, Bianca, was so sweet and pretty, and pleasant-spoken, that more than one suitor asked her father for her hand. But Baptista said the elder daughter must marry first.

So Bianca's suitors decided among themselves to try and get some one to marry Katharine--and then the father could at least be got to listen to their suit for Bianca.

A gentleman from Verona, named Petruchio, was the one they thought of, and, half in jest, they asked him if he would marry Katharine, the disagreeable scold. Much to their surprise he said yes, that was just the sort of wife for him, and if Katharine were handsome and rich, he himself would undertake soon to make her good-tempered.

Petruchio began by asking Baptista's permission to pay court to his gentle daughter Katharine--and Baptista was obliged to own that she was anything but gentle. And just then her music master rushed in, complaining that the naughty girl had broken her lute over his head, because he told her she was not playing correctly.

"Never mind," said Petruchio, "I love her better than ever, and long to have some chat with her."

When Katharine came, he said, "Good-morrow, Kate--for that, I hear, is your name."

"You've only heard half," said Katharine, rudely.

"Oh, no," said Petruchio, "they call you plain Kate, and bonny Kate, and sometimes Kate the shrew, and so, hearing your mildness praised in every town, and your beauty too, I ask you for my wife."

"Your wife!" cried Kate. "Never!" She said some extremely disagreeable things to him, and, I am sorry to say, ended by boxing his ears.

"If you do that again, I'll cuff you," he said quietly; and still protested, with many compliments, that he would marry none but her.

When Baptista came back, he asked at once--

"How speed you with my daughter?"

"How should I speed but well," replied Petruchio--"how, but well?"

"How now, daughter Katharine?" the father went on.

"I don't think," said Katharine, angrily, "you are acting a father's part in wishing me to marry this mad-cap ruffian."

"Ah!" said Petruchio, "you and all the world would talk amiss of her. You should see how kind she is to me when we are alone. In short, I will go off to Venice to buy fine things for our wedding--for--kiss me, Kate! we will be married on Sunday."

With that, Katharine flounced out of the room by one door in a violent temper, and he, laughing, went out by the other. But whether she fell in love with Petruchio, or whether she was only glad to meet a man who was not afraid of her, or whether she was flattered that, in spite of her rough words and spiteful usage, he still desired her for his wife--she did indeed marry him on Sunday, as he had sworn she should.

To vex and humble Katharine's naughty, proud

spirit, he was late at the wedding, and when he came, came wearing such shabby clothes that she was ashamed to be seen with him. His servant was dressed in the same shabby way, and the horses they rode were the sport of everyone they passed.

And, after the marriage, when should have been the wedding breakfast, Petruchio carried his wife away, not allowing her to eat or drink--saying that she was his now, and he could do as he liked with her.

And his manner was so bad, and he behaved all through his wedding in so mad and dreadful a manner, that Katharine trembled and went with him. He mounted her on a stumbling, lean, old horse, and they journeyed by rough muddy ways to Petruchio's house, he scolding and snarling all the way.

She was terribly tired when she reached her new home, but Petruchio was determined that she should neither eat nor sleep that night, for he had made up his

The Wedding Trousseau:

mind to teach his bad-tempered wife a lesson she would never forget.

So he welcomed her kindly to his house, but when supper was served he found fault with everything--the meat was burnt, he said, and ill-served, and he loved her far too much to let her eat anything but the best. At last Katharine, tired out with her journey, went supperless to bed. Then her husband, still telling her how he loved her, and how anxious he was that she should sleep well, pulled her bed to pieces, throwing the pillows and bedclothes on the floor, so that she could not go to bed at all, and still kept growling and scolding at the servants so that Kate might see how unbeautiful a thing ill-temper was.

The next day, too, Katharine's food was all found fault with, and caught away before she could touch a mouthful, and she was sick and giddy for want of sleep. Then she said to one of the servants--

"I pray thee go and get me some repast. I care not what."

"What say you to a neat's foot?" said the servant.

Katharine said "Yes," eagerly; but the servant, who was in his master's secret, said he feared it was not good for hasty-tempered people. Would she like tripe?

"Bring it me," said Katharine.

"I don't think that is good for hasty-tempered people," said the servant. "What do you say to a dish of beef and mustard?"

"I love it," said Kate.

"But mustard is too hot."

"Why, then, the beef, and let the mustard go," cried Katharine, who was getting hungrier and hungrier.

"No," said the servant, "you must have the mustard, or you get no beef from me."

"Then," cried Katharine, losing patience, "let it be both, or one, or anything thou wilt."

"Why, then," said the servant, "the mustard without the beef!"

Then Katharine saw he was making fun of her, and boxed his ears.

Just then Petruchio brought her some food--but she had scarcely begun to satisfy her hunger, before he called for the tailor to bring her new clothes, and the table was cleared, leaving her still hungry. Katharine was pleased with the pretty new dress and cap that the tailor had made for her, but Petruchio found fault with everything, flung the cap and gown on the floor vowing his dear wife should not wear any such foolish things.

"I will have them," cried Katharine. "All gentlewomen wear such caps as these--"

"When you are gentle you shall have one too," he answered, "and not till then." When he had driven away the tailor with angry words--but privately asking his friend to see him paid--Petruchio said--

"Come, Kate, let's go to your father's, shabby as we are, for as the sun breaks through the darkest clouds, so honor peereth in the meanest habit. It is about seven o'clock now. We shall easily get there by dinner-time."

"It's nearly two," said Kate, but civilly enough, for she had grown to see that she could not bully her husband, as she had done her father and her sister; "it's nearly two, and it will be supper-time before we get there."

"It shall be seven," said Petruchio, obstinately, "before I start. Why, whatever I say or do, or think, you do nothing but contradict. I won't go to-day, and before I do go, it shall be what o'clock I say it is."

At last they started for her father's house.

"Look at the moon," said he.

"It's the sun," said Katharine, and indeed it was.

"I say it is the moon. Contradicting again! It shall be sun or moon, or whatever I choose, or I won't take you to your father's."

Then Katharine gave in, once and for all. "What you will have it named," she said, "it is, and so it shall be so for Katharine." And so it was, for from that moment Katharine felt that she had met her master, and never again showed her naughty tempers to him, or anyone else.

So they journeyed on to Baptista's house, and arriving there, they found all folks keeping Bianca's wedding feast, and that of another newly married couple, Hortensio and his wife. They were made welcome, and sat down to the feast, and all was merry, save that Hortensio's wife, seeing Katharine subdued to her husband, thought she could safely say many disagreeable things, that in the old days, when Katharine was free and forward, she would not have dared to say. But Katharine answered with such spirit and such moderation, that she turned the laugh against the new bride.

After dinner, when the ladies had retired, Baptista joined in a laugh against Petruchio, saying "Now in good sadness, son Petruchio, I fear you have got the veriest shrew of all."

"You are wrong," said Petruchio, "let me prove it to you. Each of us shall send a message to his wife, desiring her to come to him, and the one whose wife comes most readily shall win a wager which we will agree on."

The others said yes readily enough, for each thought his own wife the most dutiful, and each thought he was quite sure to win the wager.

They proposed a wager of twenty crowns.

"Twenty crowns," said Petruchio, "I'll venture so much on my hawk or hound, but twenty times as much upon my wife."

"A hundred then," cried Lucentio, Bianca's husband.

"Content," cried the others.

Then Lucentio sent a message to the fair Bianca bidding her to come to him. And Baptista said he was certain his daughter would come. But the servant coming back, said--

"Sir, my mistress is busy, and she cannot come."'

"There's an answer for you," said Petruchio.

"You may think yourself fortunate if your wife does not send you a worse."

"I hope, better," Petruchio answered. Then Hortensio said--

"Go and entreat my wife to come to me at once."

"Oh--if you entreat her," said Petruchio.

"I am afraid," answered Hortensio, sharply, "do what you can, yours will not be entreated."

But now the servant came in, and said--

"She says you are playing some jest, she will not come."

"Better and better," cried Petruchio; "now go to your mistress and say I command her to come to me."

They all began to laugh, saying they knew what her answer would be, and that she would not come.

Then suddenly Baptista cried--

"Here comes Katharine!" And sure enough--there she was.

"What do you wish, sir?" she asked her husband.

"Where are your sister and Hortensio's wife?"

"Talking by the parlor fire."

"Fetch them here."

When she was gone to fetch them, Lucentio said--

"Here is a wonder!"

"I wonder what it means," said Hortensio.

"It means peace," said Petruchio, "and love, and quiet life."

"Well," said Baptista, "you have won the wager, and I will add another twenty thousand crowns to her dowry--another dowry for another daughter--for she is as changed as if she were someone else."

So Petruchio won his wager, and had in Katharine always a loving wife and true, and now he had changed her proud and angry spirit he loved her well, and there was nothing ever but love between those two. And so they lived happy ever afterwards.

Romeo & Juliet

Illustrations by Oreste Cortazzo, c1890, Ludovic Marchetti, c1890 & Lucius Rossi, c1890

Once upon a time there lived in Verona two great families named Montagu and Capulet. They were both rich, and I suppose they were as sensible, in most things, as other people. But in one thing they were extremely silly. There was an old, old quarrel between the two families, and instead of making it up like reasonable folks, they made a sort of pet of their quarrel, and would not let it die out. So that a Montagu wouldn't speak to a Capulet if he met one in the street--nor a Capulet to a Montagu--or if they did speak, it was to say rude and unpleasant things, which often ended in a fight. And their relations and servants were just as foolish, so that street fights and duels and uncomfortablenesses of that kind were always growing out of the Montagu-and-Capulet quarrel.

Now Lord Capulet, the head of that family, gave a masquerade party– a grand supper and a dance--and he was so hospitable that he said anyone might come to it except (of course) the Montagus. But there was a young Montagu named Romeo, who very much wanted to be there, because Rosaline, the lady he loved, had been asked. This lady had never been at all kind to him, and he had no reason to love her; but the fact was that he wanted to love somebody, and as he hadn't seen the right lady, he was obliged to love the wrong one. So to the Capulet's grand party he came, with his friends Mercutio and Benvolio.

Old Capulet, not recognizing Romeo in his mask, welcomed him and his two friends very kindly--and young Romeo moved about among the crowd of courtly folk dressed in their velvets and satins, the men with jeweled sword hilts and collars, and the ladies with brilliant gems on breast and arms, and stones of price set in their bright girdles. Romeo was in his best too, and though he wore a black mask over his eyes and nose, everyone could see by his mouth and his hair, and the way he held his head, that he was twelve times handsomer than anyone else in the room.

Presently amid the dancers he saw a lady so beautiful and so lovable that from that moment he never again gave one thought to that Rosaline whom he had thought he loved. And he looked at this other fair lady, as she moved in the dance in her white satin and

pearls, and all the world seemed vain and worthless to him compared with her. And he was saying this, or something like it, when Tybalt, Lady Capulet's nephew, hearing his voice, knew him to be Romeo. Tybalt, being very angry, went at once to his uncle, and told him how a Montagu had come uninvited to the feast; but old Capulet was too fine a gentleman to be discourteous to any man under his own roof, and he bade Tybalt be quiet. But this young man only waited for a chance to quarrel with Romeo.

In the meantime Romeo made his way to the fair lady, and told her in sweet words that he loved her, and kissed her. Just then her mother sent for her, and then Romeo found out that the lady on whom he had set his heart's hopes was Juliet, the daughter of Lord Capulet, his sworn foe. So he went away, sorrowing indeed, but loving her none the less.

Then Juliet said to her nurse:

"Who is that gentleman that would not dance?"

"His name is Romeo, and a Montagu, the only son of your great enemy," answered the nurse.

Then Juliet went to her room, and looked out of her window, over the beautiful green-grey garden, where the moon was shining. And Romeo was hidden in that garden among the trees--because he could not bear to go right away without trying to see her again.
So she--not knowing him to be there--spoke her secret thought aloud, and told the quiet garden how she loved Romeo.

And Romeo heard and was glad beyond measure. Hidden below, he looked up and saw her fair face in the moonlight, framed in the blossoming creepers that grew round her window, and as he looked and listened, he felt as though he had been carried away in a dream, and set down by some magician in that beautiful and enchanted garden.

"Ah--why are you called Romeo?" said Juliet. "Since I love you, what does it matter what you are called?"

"Call me but love, and I'll be new baptized--henceforth I never will be Romeo," he cried, stepping into the full white moonlight from the shade of the cypresses and oleanders that had hidden him.

She was frightened at first, but when she saw that it was Romeo himself, and no stranger,

she too was glad, and, he standing in the garden below and she leaning from the window, they spoke long together, each one trying to find the sweetest words in the world, to make that pleasant talk that lovers use. And the tale of all they said, and the sweet music their voices made together, is all set down in a golden book, where you children may read it for yourselves some day.

And the time passed so quickly, as it does for folk who love each other and are together, that when the time came to part, it seemed as though they had met but that moment-- and indeed they hardly knew how to part.

"I will send to you to-morrow," said Juliet.

And so at last, with lingering and longing, they said good-bye.

Juliet went into her room, and a dark curtain hid her bright window. Romeo went away through the still and dewy garden like a man in a dream.

The next morning, very early, Romeo went to Friar Laurence, a priest, and, telling him all the story, begged him to marry him to Juliet without delay. And this, after some talk, the priest consented to do.

So when Juliet sent her old nurse to Romeo that day to know what he purposed to do, the old woman took back a message that all was well, and all things ready for the marriage of Juliet and Romeo on the next morning.

The young lovers were afraid to ask their parents' consent to their marriage, as young people should do, because of this foolish old quarrel between the Capulets and the Montagues.

And Friar Laurence was willing to help the young lovers secretly, because he thought that when they were once married their parents might soon be told, and that the match might put a happy end to the old quarrel.

So the next morning early, Romeo and Juliet were married at Friar Laurence's cell, and parted with tears and kisses. And Romeo promised to come into the garden that evening, and the nurse got ready a rope-ladder to let down from the window, so that Romeo could climb up and talk to his dear wife quietly and alone.

But that very day a dreadful thing happened.

Tybalt, the young man who had been so vexed at Romeo's going to the Capulet's feast, met him and his two friends, Mercutio and Benvolio, in the street, called Romeo a villain, and asked him to fight. Romeo had no wish to fight with Juliet's cousin, but Mercutio drew his sword, and he and Tybalt fought. And Mercutio was killed. When Romeo saw that this friend was dead, he forgot everything except anger at the man who had killed him, and he and Tybalt fought till Tybalt fell dead.

So, on the very day of his wedding, Romeo killed his dear Juliet's cousin, and was sentenced to be banished. Poor Juliet and her young husband met that night indeed; he climbed the rope-ladder among the flowers, and found her window, but their meeting was a sad one, and they parted with bitter tears and hearts heavy, because they could not know when they should meet again.

Now Juliet's father, who, of course, had no idea that she was married, wished her to wed a gentleman named Paris, and was so angry when she refused, that she hurried away to ask Friar Laurence what she should do. He advised her to pretend to consent, and then he said:

"I will give you a draught that will make you seem to be dead for two days, and then when they take you to church it will be to bury you, and not to marry you. They will put you in the vault thinking you are dead, and before you wake up Romeo and I will be there to take care of you. Will you do this, or are you afraid?"

"I will do it; talk not to me of fear!" said Juliet. And she went home and told her father she would marry Paris. If she had spoken out and told her father the truth . . . well, then this would have been a different story.

Lord Capulet was very much pleased to get his own way, and set about inviting his friends and getting the wedding feast ready. Everyone stayed up all night, for there was a great deal to do, and very little time to do it in. Lord Capulet was anxious to get Juliet married because he saw she was very unhappy. Of course she was really fretting about her husband Romeo, but her father thought she was grieving for the death of her cousin Tybalt, and he thought marriage would give her something else to think about.

Early in the morning the nurse came to call Juliet, and to dress her for her wedding; but she would not wake, and at last the nurse cried out suddenly--

"Alas! alas! help! help! my lady's dead!"

Lady Capulet came running in, and then Lord Capulet, and Lord Paris, the bridegroom. There lay Juliet cold and white and lifeless, and all their weeping could not wake her. So it was a burying that day instead of a marrying. Meantime Friar Laurence had sent a messenger to Mantua, where Romeo was in exile, a letter telling him of all these things; and all would have been well, only the messenger was delayed, and could not go.

But ill news travels fast. Romeo's servant who knew the secret of the marriage, but not of Juliet's pretended death, heard of her funeral, and hurried to Mantua to tell Romeo how his young wife was dead and lying in the grave.

"Is it so?" cried Romeo, heart-broken. "Then I will lie by Juliet's side to-night."

And he bought himself a poison, and went straight back to Verona. He hastened to the tomb where Juliet was lying. It was not a grave, but a vault. He broke open the door, and was just going down the stone steps that led to the vault where all the dead Capulets lay, when he heard a voice behind him calling on him to stop.

It was the Count Paris, who was to have married Juliet that very day.

"How dare you come here and disturb the dead bodies of the Capulets, you vile Montagu?" cried Paris.

Poor Romeo, half mad with sorrow, yet tried to answer gently.

"You were told," said Paris, "that if you returned to Verona you must die."

"I must indeed," said Romeo. "I came here for nothing else. Good, gentle youth--leave me! Oh, go--before I do

you any harm! I love you better than myself--go--leave me here--"

Then Paris said, "I defy you, and I arrest you as a felon," and Romeo, in his anger and despair, drew his sword. They fought, and Paris was killed.

As Romeo's sword pierced him, Paris cried--

"Oh, I am slain! If thou be merciful, open the tomb, and lay me with Juliet!"

And Romeo said, "In faith I will."

And he carried the dead man into the tomb and laid him by the dear Juliet's side. Then he kneeled by Juliet and spoke to her, and held her in his arms, and kissed her cold lips, believing that she was dead, while all the while she was coming nearer and nearer to the time of her awakening. Then he drank the poison, and died beside his sweetheart and wife.

Now came Friar Laurence when it was too late, and saw all that had happened--and then poor Juliet woke out of her sleep to find her husband and her friend both dead beside her.

The noise of the fight had brought other folks to the place too, and Friar Laurence, hearing them, ran away, and Juliet was left alone. She saw the cup that had held the poison, and knew how all had happened, and since no poison was left for her, she drew her Romeo's dagger and thrust it through her heart--and so, falling with her head on her Romeo's breast, she died. And here ends the story of these faithful and most unhappy lovers.

And when the old folks knew from Friar Laurence of all that had befallen, they sorrowed exceedingly, and now, seeing all the mischief their wicked quarrel had wrought, they repented them of it, and over the bodies of their dead children they clasped hands at last, in friendship and forgiveness.

Much Ado About Nothing

**Illustrations by N.M. Price, 1905,
Willy Pogany, 1949 & L.E. Wright, 1909**

In Sicily is a town called Messina, which is the scene of a curious storm in a teacup that raged several hundred years ago.

It began with sunshine. Don Pedro, Prince of Arragon, in Spain, had gained so complete a victory over his foes that the very land whence they came is forgotten. Feeling happy and playful after the fatigues of war, Don Pedro came for a holiday to Messina, and in his group were his stepbrother Don John and two young Italian lords,

Benedick and Claudio.

Benedick was a merry chatterbox, who had determined to live a bachelor. Claudio, on the other hand, no sooner arrived at Messina than he fell in love with Hero, the daughter of Leonato, Governor of Messina.

One July day, a perfumer called Borachio was working in Leonato's house, when the sound of conversation floated through the open window.

"Give me your candid opinion of Hero," Claudio, asked, and Borachio, unseen, settled himself for comfortable listening.

"Too short and brown for praise," was Benedick's reply; "but alter her color or height, and you spoil her."

"In my eyes she is the sweetest of women," said Claudio.

"Not in mine," retorted Benedick, "and I have no need for glasses. She is like the last day of December compared with the first of May if you set her beside her cousin. Unfortunately, the Lady Beatrice is a fury."

Beatrice was Leonato's niece. She amused herself by saying witty and severe things about Benedick, who called her Dear Lady Disdain. She was wont to say that she was born under a dancing star, and could not therefore be dull.

Claudio and Benedick were still talking when Don Pedro came up and said good-humoredly, "Well, gentlemen, what's the secret?"

"I am longing," answered Benedick, "for your Grace to command me to tell."

"I charge you, then, on your allegiance to tell me," said Don Pedro, falling in with his humor.

"I can be as dumb as a mute," apologized Benedick to Claudio, "but his Grace commands my speech." To Don Pedro he said, "Claudio is in love with Hero, Leonato's short daughter."

Don Pedro was pleased, for he admired Hero and was fond of Claudio. When Benedick had departed, he said to Claudio, "Be steadfast in your love for Hero, and I will help you to win her. To-night her father gives a masquerade, and I will pretend I am Claudio, and tell her how Claudio loves her, and if she be pleased, I will go to her father and ask his consent to your union."

Most men like to do their own wooing, but if you fall in love with a Governor's only daughter, you are fortunate if you can trust a prince to plead for you.

Claudio then was fortunate, but he was unfortunate as well, for he had an enemy who was outwardly a friend. This enemy was Don Pedro's stepbrother Don John, who was jealous of Claudio because Don Pedro preferred him to Don John.

It was to Don John that Borachio came with the interesting conversation which he had overheard.

"I shall have some fun at that masquerade myself," said Don John when Borachio ceased speaking.

On the night of the masquerade, Don Pedro, masked and pretending he was Claudio, asked Hero if he might walk with her.

They moved away together, and Don John went up to Claudio and said, "Signor Benedick, I believe?" "The same," fibbed Claudio.

"I should be much obliged then," said Don John, "if you would use your influence with my brother to cure him of his love for Hero. She is beneath him in rank."

"How do you know he loves her?" inquired Claudio.

"I heard him swear his affection," was the reply, and Borachio chimed in with, "So did I too."

Claudio was then left to himself, and his thought was that his Prince had betrayed him. "Farewell, Hero," he muttered; "I was a fool to trust to an agent."

Meanwhile Beatrice and Benedick (who was masked) were having a brisk exchange of opinions.

"Did Benedick ever make you laugh?" asked she.

"Who is Benedick?" he inquired.

"A Prince's jester," replied Beatrice, and she spoke so sharply that "I would not marry her," he declared afterwards, "if her estate were the Garden of Eden."

But the principal speaker at the masquerade was neither Beatrice nor Benedick. It was Don Pedro, who carried out his plan to the letter, and brought the light back to Claudio's face in a twinkling, by appearing before him with Leonato and Hero, and saying, "Claudio, when would you like to go to church?"

"To-morrow," was the prompt answer. "Time goes on crutches till I marry Hero."

"Give her a week, my dear son," said Leonato, and Claudio's heart thumped with joy.

"And now," said the amiable Don Pedro, "we must find a wife for Signor Benedick. It is a task for Hercules."

"I will help you," said Leonato, "if I have to sit up ten nights."

Then Hero spoke. "I will do what I can, my lord, to find a good husband for Beatrice."

Thus, with happy laughter, ended the masquerade which had given Claudio a lesson for nothing.

Borachio cheered up Don John by laying a plan before him with which he was confident he could persuade both Claudio and Don Pedro that Hero was a fickle girl who had two strings to her bow. Don John agreed to this plan of hate.

Don Pedro, on the other hand, had devised a cunning plan of love. "If," he said to Leonato, "we pretend, when Beatrice is near enough to overhear us, that Benedick is pining for her love, she will pity him, see his good qualities, and love him. And if, when Benedick thinks we don't know he is listening, we say how sad it is that the beautiful Beatrice should be in love with a heartless scoffer like Benedick, he will certainly be on his knees before her in a week or less."

So one day, when Benedick was reading in a summerhouse, Claudio sat down outside it with Leonato, and said, "Your daughter told me something about a letter she wrote."

"Letter!" exclaimed Leonato. "She will get up twenty times in the night and write goodness knows what. But once Hero peeped, and saw the words 'Benedick and Beatrice' on the sheet, and then Beatrice tore it up."

"Hero told me," said Claudio, "that she cried, 'O sweet Benedick!'"

Benedick was touched to the core by this improbable story, which he was vain enough to believe. "She is fair and good," he said to himself. "I must not seem proud. I feel that I love her. People will laugh, of course; but their paper bullets will do me no harm."

At this moment Beatrice came to the summerhouse, and said, "Against my will, I have come to tell you that dinner is ready."

"Fair Beatrice, I thank you," said Benedick.

"I took no more pains to come than you take pains to thank me," was the rejoinder, intended to freeze him.

But it did not freeze him. It warmed him. The meaning he squeezed out of her rude speech was that she was delighted to come to him.

Hero, who had undertaken the task of melting the heart of Beatrice, took no trouble to seek an occasion. She simply said to her maid Margaret one day, "Run into the parlor and whisper to Beatrice that Ursula and I are talking about her in the orchard."

Having said this, she felt as sure that Beatrice would overhear what was meant for her

ears as if she had made an appointment with her cousin.

In the orchard was a bower, screened from the sun by honeysuckles, and Beatrice entered it a few minutes after Margaret had gone on her errand.

"But are you sure," asked Ursula, who was one of Hero's attendants, "that Benedick loves Beatrice so devotedly?"

"So say the Prince and my betrothed," replied Hero, "and they wished me to tell her, but I said, 'No! Let Benedick get over it.'"

"Why did you say that?"

"Because Beatrice is unbearably proud. Her eyes sparkle with disdain and scorn. She is too conceited to love. I should not like to see her making game of poor Benedick's love. I would rather see Benedick waste away like a covered fire."

"I don't agree with you," said Ursula. "I think your cousin is too clear-sighted not to see the merits of Benedick." "He is the one man in Italy, except Claudio," said Hero.

The talkers then left the orchard, and Beatrice, excited and tender, stepped out of the summer-house, saying to herself, "Poor dear Benedick, be true to me, and your love shall tame this wild heart of mine."

We now return to the plan of hate.

The night before the day fixed for Claudio's wedding, Don John entered a room in which Don Pedro and Claudio were conversing, and asked Claudio if he intended to be married to-morrow.

"You know he does!" said Don Pedro.

"He may know differently," said Don John, "when he has seen what I will show him if he will follow me."

They followed him into the garden; and they saw a lady leaning out of Hero's window talking love to Borachio.

Claudio thought the lady was Hero, and said, "I will shame her for it to-morrow!" Don Pedro thought she was Hero, too; but she was not Hero; she was Margaret.

Don John chuckled noiselessly when Claudio and Don Pedro quitted the garden; he gave Borachio a purse containing a thousand ducats.

The money made Borachio feel very gay, and when he was walking in the street with his friend Conrade, he boasted of his wealth and the giver, and told what he had done.

A watchman overheard them, and thought that a man who had been paid a thousand ducats for villainy was worth taking in charge. He therefore arrested Borachio and Conrade, who spent the rest of the night in prison.

Before noon of the next day half the aristocrats in Messina were at church. Hero thought it was her wedding day, and she was there in her wedding dress, no cloud on her pretty face or in her frank and shining eyes.

The priest was Friar Francis.

Turning to Claudio, he said, "You come hither, my lord, to marry this lady?" "No!" contradicted Claudio.

Leonato thought he was quibbling over grammar. "You should have said, Friar," said he, "'You come to be married to her.'"

Friar Francis turned to Hero. "Lady," he said, "you come hither to be married to this Count?" "I do," replied Hero.

"If either of you know any impediment to this marriage, I charge you to utter it," said the Friar.

"Do you know of any, Hero?" asked Claudio. "None," said she.

"Know you of any, Count?" demanded the Friar. "I dare reply for him, 'None,'" said Leonato.

Claudio exclaimed bitterly, "O! what will not men dare say! Father," he continued, "will you give me your daughter?" "As freely," replied Leonato, "as God gave her to me."

"And what can I give you," asked Claudio, "which is worthy of this gift?" "Nothing," said Don Pedro, "unless you give the gift back to the giver."

"Sweet Prince, you teach me," said Claudio. "There, Leonato, take her back."

These brutal words were followed by others which flew from Claudio, Don Pedro and Don John.

The church seemed no longer sacred. Hero took her own part as long as she could, then she swooned. All her persecutors left the church, except her father, who was befooled by the accusations against her, and cried, "Hence from her! Let her die!"

But Friar Francis saw Hero blameless with his clear eyes that probed the soul. "She is innocent," he said; "a thousand signs have told me so."

Hero revived under his kind gaze. Her father, flurried and angry, knew not what to think, and the Friar said, "They have left her as one dead with shame. Let us pretend that she is dead until the truth is declared, and slander turns to remorse."

"The Friar advises well," said Benedick. Then Hero was led away into a retreat, and Beatrice and Benedick remained alone in the church.

Benedick knew she had been weeping bitterly and long. "Surely I do believe your fair cousin is wronged," he said. She still wept.

"Is it not strange," asked Benedick, gently, "that I love nothing in the world as well as you?"

"It were as possible for me to say I loved nothing as well as you," said Beatrice, "but I do not say it. I am sorry for my cousin."

"Tell me what to do for her," said Benedick. "Kill Claudio."

"Ha! not for the wide world," said Benedick. "Your refusal kills me," said Beatrice. "Farewell."

"Enough! I will challenge him," cried Benedick.

During this scene Borachio and Conrade were in prison. There they were examined by a constable called Dogberry.

The watchman gave evidence to the effect that Borachio had said that he had received a thousand ducats for conspiring against Hero.

Leonato was not present at this examination, but he was nevertheless now thoroughly

convinced Of Hero's innocence. He played the part of bereaved father very well, and when Don Pedro and Claudio called on him in a friendly way, he said to the Italian, "You have slandered my child to death, and I challenge you to combat."

"I cannot fight an old man," said Claudio.

"You could kill a girl," sneered Leonato, and Claudio crimsoned.

Hot words grew from hot words, and both Don Pedro and Claudio were feeling scorched when Leonato left the room and Benedick entered.

"The old man," said Claudio, "was like to have snapped my nose off."

"You are a villain!" said Benedick, shortly. "Fight me when and with what weapon you please, or I call you a coward."

Claudio was astounded, but said, "I'll meet you. Nobody shall say I can't carve a calf's head."

Benedick smiled, and as it was time for Don Pedro to receive officials, the Prince sat down in a chair of state and prepared his mind for justice.

The door soon opened to admit Dogberry and his prisoners.

"What offence," said Don Pedro, "are these men charged with?"

Borachio thought the moment a happy one for making a clean breast of it. He laid the whole blame on Don John, who had disappeared. "The lady Hero being dead," he said, "I desire nothing but the reward of a murderer."

Claudio heard with anguish and deep repentance.

Upon the re-entrance of Leonato he said to him, "This slave makes clear your daughter's innocence. Choose your revenge.

"Leonato," said Don Pedro, humbly, "I am ready for any penance you may impose."

"I ask you both, then," said Leonato, "to proclaim my daughter's innocence, and to honor her tomb by singing her praise before it. As for you, Claudio, I have this to say: my brother has a daughter so like Hero that she might be a copy of her. Marry her, and my vengeful

feelings die."

"Noble sir," said Claudio, "I am yours." Claudio then went to his room and composed a solemn song. Going to the church with Don Pedro and his attendants, he sang it before the monument of Leonato's family. When he had ended he said, "Good night, Hero. Yearly will I do this."

He then gravely, as became a gentleman whose heart was Hero's, made ready to marry a girl whom he did not love. He was told to meet her in Leonato's house, and was faithful to his appointment.

He was shown into a room where Antonio (Leonato's brother) and several masked ladies entered after him. Friar Francis, Leonato, and Benedick were present.

Antonio led one of the ladies towards Claudio.

"Sweet," said the young man, "let me see your face."

"Swear first to marry her," said Leonato.

"Give me your hand," said Claudio to the lady; "before this holy friar I swear to marry you if you will be my wife."

"Alive I was your wife," said the lady, as she drew off her mask.

"Another Hero!" exclaimed Claudio.

"Hero died," explained Leonato, "only while slander lived."

The Friar was then going to marry the reconciled pair, but Benedick interrupted him with, "Softly, Friar; which of these ladies is Beatrice?"

Then was Beatrice unmasked, and Benedick said, "You love me, don't you?"

"Only moderately," was the reply. "Do you love me?"

"Moderately," answered Benedick.

"I was told you were well-nigh dead for me," remarked Beatrice.

"Of you I was told the same," said Benedick.

"Here's your own hand in evidence of your love," said Claudio, producing a feeble sonnet which Benedick had written to his sweetheart. "And here," said Hero, "is a tribute to Benedick, which I picked out of the pocket of Beatrice."

"A miracle!" exclaimed Benedick. "Our hands are against our hearts! Come, I will marry you, Beatrice."

"You shall be my husband to save your life," was the rejoinder.

Benedick kissed her on the mouth; and the Friar married them after he had married Claudio and Hero.

"How is Benedick the married man?" asked Don Pedro.

"Too happy to be made unhappy," replied Benedick. "Crack what jokes you will. As for you, Claudio, I had hoped to run you through the body, but as you are now my kinsman, live whole and love my cousin."

"My cudgel was in love with you, Benedick, until to-day," said Claudio; but, "Come, come, let's dance," said Benedick.

And dance they did. Not even the news of the capture of Don John was able to stop the flying feet of the happy lovers, for revenge is not sweet against an evil man who has failed to do harm.

BE YOU BLITHE AND BONNY

A Midsummer Night's Dream

Illustrations by Arthur Rackham, 1908

Hermia and Lysander were lovers; but Hermia's father wished her to marry another man, named Demetrius.

Now, in Athens, where they lived, there was a wicked law, by which any girl who refused to marry according to her father's wishes, might be put to death. Hermia's father was so angry with her for refusing to do as he wished, that he actually brought her before the Duke of Athens, Theseus, to ask that she might be killed, if she still refused to obey him. The Duke who himself is engaged to be married, gave her four days to think about it.

Lysander of course was nearly mad with grief, and the best thing to do seemed to him for Hermia to run away to his aunt's house at a place beyond the reach of that cruel law; and there he would come to her and marry her. But before she started, she told her friend, Helena, what she was going to do.

Helena had been Demetrius' sweetheart long before his marriage with Hermia had been thought of, and being very silly, like all jealous people, she could not see that it was not poor Hermia's fault that Demetrius wished to marry her instead of his own lady, Helena. She knew that if she told Demetrius that Hermia was going, as she was, to the wood outside Athens, he would follow her, "and I can follow him, and at least I shall see him," she said to herself. So she went to him, and betrayed her friend's secret.

Now this wood where Lysander was to meet Hermia, and where the other two had decided to follow them, was full of fairies, as most woods are, if one only had the eyes to see them, and in this wood on this night were the King and Queen of the fairies, Oberon and Titania. Now fairies are very wise people, but now and then they can be quite as foolish as mortal folk. Oberon and Titania, who might have been as happy as the days were long, had thrown away all their joy in a foolish quarrel. They never met without saying disagreeable things to each other, and scolded each other so dreadfully that all their little fairy followers, for fear, would creep into acorn cups and hide them there.

So, instead of keeping one happy Court and dancing all night through in the moonlight as is fairies' use, the King with his attendants wandered through one part of the wood, while the Queen with hers kept state in another. And the cause of all this trouble was a little boy whom Titania had taken to be one of her followers. Oberon wanted the child to follow him and be one of his fairy knights; but the Queen would not give him up.

On this night, in a mossy moonlit glade, the King and Queen of the fairies met.

"Ill met by moonlight, proud Titania," said the King.

"What! jealous, Oberon?" answered the Queen. "You spoil everything with your quarreling. Come, fairies, let us leave him. I am not friends with him now."

"It rests with you to make up the quarrel," said the King.

"Give me that little boy, and I will again be your humble servant and suitor."

"Set your mind at rest," said the Queen. "Your whole fairy kingdom buys not that boy from me. Come, fairies."

And she and her train rode off down the moonbeams.

"Well, go your ways," said Oberon. "But I'll be even with you before you leave this wood."

Then Oberon called his favorite fairy, Puck. Puck was the spirit of mischief. He used to slip into the dairies and take the cream away, and get into the churn so that the butter would not come, and turn the beer sour, and lead people out of their way on dark nights and then laugh at them, and tumble people's stools from under them when they were going to sit down, and upset their hot ale over their chins when they were going to drink.

"Now," said Oberon to this little sprite, "fetch me the flower called Love-in-idleness. The juice of that little purple flower laid on the eyes of those who sleep will make them, when they wake, love the first thing they see. I will put some of the juice of that flower on my Titania's eyes, and when she wakes she will love the first thing she sees, were it lion, bear, or wolf, or bull, or meddling monkey, or a busy ape."

While Puck was gone, Demetrius passed through the glade followed by poor Helena, and still she told him how she loved him and reminded him of all his promises, and still he told

her that he did not and could not love her, and that his promises were nothing. Oberon was sorry for poor Helena, and when Puck returned with the flower, he bade him follow Demetrius and put some of the juice on his eyes, so that he might love Helena when he woke and looked on her, as much as she loved him. So Puck set off, and wandering through the wood found, not Demetrius, but Lysander, on whose eyes he put the juice; but when Lysander woke, he saw not his own Hermia, but Helena, who was walking through the wood looking for the cruel Demetrius; and directly he saw her he loved her and left his own lady, as he was under the spell of the purple flower.

When Hermia woke she found Lysander gone, and wandered about the wood trying to find him. Puck went back and told Oberon what he had done, and Oberon soon found that he had made a mistake, and set about looking for Demetrius, and having found him, put some of the juice on his eyes. And the first thing Demetrius saw when he woke was also Helena. So now Demetrius and Lysander were both following her through the wood, and it was Hermia's turn to follow her lover as Helena had done before. The end of it was that Helena and Hermia began to quarrel, and Demetrius and Lysander went off to fight. Oberon was very sorry to see his kind scheme to help these lovers turn out so

badly. So he said to Puck--

"These two young men are going to fight. You must overhang the night with drooping fog, and lead them so astray, that one will never find the other. When they are tired out, they will fall asleep. Then drop this other herb on Lysander's eyes. That will give him his old sight and his old love. Then each man will have the lady who loves him, and they will all think that this has been only a Midsummer Night's Dream. Then when this is done, all will be well with them."

So Puck went and did as he was told, and when the two had fallen asleep without meeting each other, Puck poured the juice on Lysander's eyes, and said:--

"When thou wakest, Thou takest True delight In the sight Of thy former lady's eye: Jack shall have Jill; Nought shall go ill."

Meanwhile Oberon found Titania asleep on a bank where grew wild thyme, oxlips, and violets, and woodbine, musk-roses and eglantine. There Titania always slept a part of the night, wrapped in the enameled skin of a snake. Oberon stooped over her and laid the juice on her eyes, saying:--

"What thou seest when thou wake, Do it for thy true love take."

Now, it happened that when Titania woke the first thing she saw was a silly man, one of a party of players who had come out into the wood to rehearse their play. This clown had met with Puck, who had clapped an ass's head on his shoulders so that it looked as if it grew there. Directly Titania woke and saw this dreadful monster, she said, "What angel is this? Are you as wise as you are beautiful?"

"If I am wise enough to find my way out of this wood, that's enough for me," said the foolish man.

"Do not desire to go out of the wood," said Titania. The spell of the love-juice was on her, and to her the man seemed the most beautiful and delightful creature on all the earth. "I love you," she went on. "Come with me, and I will give you fairies to attend on you."

So she called four fairies, whose names were Peaseblossom, Cobweb, Moth, and Mustardseed.

"You must attend this gentleman," said the Queen. "Feed him with apricots and dewberries, purple grapes, green figs, and mulberries. Steal honey-bags for him from the bumble-bees, and with the wings of painted butterflies fan the moonbeams from his sleeping eyes."

"I will," said one of the fairies, and all the others said, "I will."

"Now, sit down with me," said the Queen to the man, "and let me stroke your dear cheeks, and stick musk-roses in your smooth, sleek head, and kiss your fair large ears, my gentle joy."

"Where's Peaseblossom?" asked the man with the ass's head. He did not care much about the Queen's affection, but he was very proud of having fairies to wait on him. "Ready," said Peaseblossom.

"Scratch my head, Peaseblossom," he said. "Where's Cobweb?" "Ready," said Cobweb.

"Bring me the honey-bag from the red bumble-bee on the top of the thistle yonder. Where's Mustardseed?"

"Ready," said Mustardseed.

"Oh, I want nothing," said the clown. "Only just help Peaseblossom to scratch. I must go to the barber's, for methinks I am marvelous hairy about the face."

"Would you like anything to eat?" said the fairy Queen.

"I should like some good dry oats," said the clown--for his donkey's head made him desire donkey's food--"and some hay to follow."

"Shall some of my fairies fetch you new nuts from the squirrel's house?" asked the Queen.

"I'd rather have a handful or two of good dried peas," said the clown. "But please don't let any of your people disturb me; I am going to sleep."

Then said the Queen, "And I will wind thee in my arms."

And so when Oberon came along he found his beautiful Queen lavishing kisses and endearments on a funny man with a donkey's head.

And before he released her from the enchantment, he persuaded her to give him the little

boy he so much desired to have. Then he took pity on her, and threw some juice of the disenchanting flower on her pretty eyes; and then in a moment she saw plainly the donkey-headed man she had been loving, and knew how foolish she had been.

Oberon took off the ass's head from the man, and left him to finish his sleep with his own silly head lying on the thyme and violets.

Thus all was made plain and straight again. Oberon and Titania loved each other more than ever. Demetrius thought of no one but Helena, and Helena had never had any thought of anyone but Demetrius.

As for Hermia and Lysander, they were as loving a couple as you could meet in a day's march, even through a fairy wood.

So the four mortal lovers, having been found by Theseus and his bride to be, went back to Athens where all three couples were married; and the fairy King and Queen live happily together in that very wood at this very day.

FRIENDS:

Merchant of Venice

Illustrations by R. André, 1881

Antonio was a rich and prosperous merchant of Venice. His ships were on nearly every sea, and he traded with Portugal, with Mexico, with England, and with India. Although proud of his riches, he was very generous with them, and delighted to use them in relieving the wants of his friends, among whom his relation, Bassanio, held the first place.

Now Bassanio, like many another gallant gentleman, was reckless and extravagant, and finding that he had not only come to the end of his fortune, but was also unable to pay his creditors, he went to Antonio for further help.

"To you, Antonio," he said, "I owe the most in money and in love: and I have thought of a plan to pay everything I owe if you will but help me."

"Say what I can do, and it shall be done," answered his friend.

Then said Bassanio, "In Belmont is a lady richly left, and from all quarters of the globe renowned suitors come to woo her, not only because she is rich, but because she is beautiful and good as well. She looked on me with such favor when last we met, that I feel sure that I should win her away from all rivals for her love had I but the means to go to Belmont, where she lives."

"All my fortunes," said Antonio, "are at sea, and so I have no ready money; but luckily my credit is good in Venice, and I will borrow for you what you need."

There was living in Venice at this time a rich money-lender, named Shylock. Antonio despised and disliked this man very much, and treated him with the greatest harshness and scorn. Shylock submitted to his indignities with a patient shrug; but deep in his heart he cherished a desire for revenge on the rich, smug merchant. For Antonio both hurt his pride and injured his business. "But for him," thought Shylock, "I should be richer by half a million ducats. On the market place, and wherever he can, he denounces the rate of interest I charge, and--worse than that--he lends out money freely."

So when Bassanio came to him to ask for a loan of three thousand ducats to Antonio for three months, Shylock hid his hatred, and turning to Antonio, said--"Harshly as you have treated me, I would be friends with you and have your love. So I will lend you the money and charge you no interest. But, just for fun, you shall sign a bond in which it shall be agreed that if you do not repay me in three months' time, then I shall have the right to a pound of your flesh, to be cut from what part of your body I choose."

"No," cried Bassanio to his friend, "you shall run no such risk for me."

"Why, fear not," said Antonio, "my ships will be home a month before the time. I will sign the bond."

Thus Bassanio was furnished with the means to go to Belmont, there to woo the lovely Portia. The very night he started, the money-lender's pretty daughter, Jessica, ran away from her father's house with her lover, and she took with her from her father's hoards some bags of ducats and precious stones. Shylock's grief and anger were terrible to see. His love for her changed to hate. "I would she were dead at my feet and the jewels in her ear," he cried. His only comfort now was in hearing of the serious losses which had befallen Antonio, some of whose ships were wrecked. "Let him look to his bond," said Shylock, "let him look to his bond."

Meanwhile Bassanio had reached Belmont, and had visited the fair Portia. He found, as he had told Antonio, that the rumor of her wealth and beauty had drawn to her suitors from far and near. But to all of them Portia had but one reply. She would only accept that suitor who would pledge himself to abide by the terms of her father's will. These were conditions that frightened away many an ardent wooer. For he who would win Portia's heart and hand, had to guess which of three caskets held her portrait. If he guessed aright, then Portia would be his bride; if wrong, then he was bound by oath never to reveal which casket he chose, never to marry, and to go away at once.

The caskets were of gold, silver, and lead. The gold one bore this inscription:--"Who chooseth me shall gain what many men desire;" the silver one had this:--"Who chooseth me shall get as much as he deserves;" while on the lead one were these words:--"Who chooseth me must give and hazard all he hath." The Prince of Morocco was among the first to submit to this test. He chose the gold casket, for he said neither base lead nor silver could contain her picture. So be chose the gold casket, and found inside the likeness of what many men desire--death.

After him came the haughty Prince of Arragon, and saying, "Let me have what I deserve--surely I deserve the lady," he chose the silver one, and found inside a fool's head. "Did I deserve no more than a fool's head?" he cried.

Then at last came Bassanio, and Portia would have delayed him from making his choice from very fear of his choosing wrong. For she loved him dearly, even as he loved her. "But," said Bassanio, "let me choose at once, for, as I am, I live upon the rack."

Then Portia bade her servants to bring music and play while her gallant lover made his choice. And Bassanio took the oath and walked up to the caskets--the musicians playing softly the while. "Mere outward show," he said, "is to be despised. The world is still deceived with ornament, and so no gaudy gold or shining silver for me. I choose the lead

casket; joy be the consequence!" And opening it, he found fair Portia's portrait inside, and he turned to her and asked if it were true that she was his.

"Yes," said Portia, "I am yours, and this house is yours, and with them I give you this ring, from which you must never part."

And Bassanio, saying that he could hardly speak for joy, found words to swear that he would never part with the ring while he lived.

Then suddenly all his happiness was dashed with sorrow, for messengers came from Venice to tell him that Antonio was ruined, and that Shylock demanded from the Duke the fulfilment of the bond, under which he was entitled to a pound of the merchant's flesh. Portia was as grieved as Bassanio to hear of the danger which threatened his friend.

"First," she said, "take me to church and make me your wife, and then go to Venice at once to help your friend. You shall take with you money enough to pay his debt twenty times over."

But when her newly-made husband had gone, Portia went after him, and arrived in Venice disguised as a lawyer, and with an introduction from a celebrated lawyer Bellario, whom the Duke of Venice had called in to decide the legal questions raised by Shylock's claim to a pound of Antonio's flesh. When the Court met, Bassanio offered Shylock twice the money borrowed, if he would withdraw his claim. But the money-lender's only answer was--

"If every ducat in six thousand ducats– Were in six parts, and every part a ducat,– I would not draw them,– I would have my bond."

It was then that Portia arrived in her disguise, and not even her own husband knew her. The Duke gave her welcome on account of the great Bellario's introduction, and left the settlement of the case to her. Then in noble words she bade Shylock have mercy. But he was deaf to her entreaties. "I will have the pound of flesh," was his reply.

"What have you to say?" asked Portia of the merchant.

"But little," he answered; "I am armed and well prepared."

"The Court awards you a pound of Antonio's flesh," said Portia to the money-lender.

"Most righteous judge!" cried Shylock. "A sentence: come, prepare."

"Tarry a little. This bond gives you no right to Antonio's blood, only to his flesh. If, then, you spill a drop of his blood, all your property will be forfeited to the State. Such is the Law."

And Shylock, in his fear, said, "Then I will take Bassanio's offer."

"No," said Portia sternly, "you shall have nothing but your bond. Take your pound of flesh, but remember, that if you take more or less, even by the weight of a hair, you will lose your property and your life."

Shylock now grew very much frightened. "Give me my three thousand ducats that I lent him, and let him go."

Bassanio would have paid it to him, but said Portia, "No! He shall have nothing but his bond."

"You, a foreigner," she added, "have sought to take the life of a Venetian citizen, and thus by the Venetian law, your life and goods are forfeited. Down, therefore, and beg mercy of the Duke."

Thus were the tables turned, and no mercy would have been shown to Shylock had it not been for Antonio. As it was, the money-lender forfeited half his fortune to the State, and he had to settle the other half on his daughter's husband, and with this he had to be content.

Bassanio, in his gratitude to the clever lawyer, was induced to part with the ring his wife had given him, and with which he had promised never to part, and when on his return to Belmont he confessed as much to Portia, she seemed very angry, and vowed she would not be friends with him until she had her ring again. But at last she told him that it was she who, in the disguise of the lawyer, had saved his friend's life, and got the ring from him. So Bassanio was forgiven, and made happier than ever, to know how rich a prize he had drawn in the lottery of the caskets.